Tilly Tiptoes and the
Gala Show

Tilly Tiptoes
and the
Gala Show

Caroline Plaisted

Illustrated by Hollie Jacobs

Catnip

CATNIP BOOKS
Published by Catnip Publishing Ltd
14 Greville Street
London EC1N 8SB

This edition first published 2011
1 3 5 7 9 10 8 6 4 2

Text © 2011 Caroline Plaisted
Illustrations © 2011 Hollie Jacobs

A CIP catalogue record for this book is available from the British Library.

ISBN 978-1-84647-135-3

Printed in Poland

www.catnippublishing.co.uk

Always remembering my parents,
Ronald and Patricia

Chapter One

It was Saturday morning and I was telling Jessie all about the ballet exam I was about to take. Jessie is my godmother and wardrobe mistress of the Grand Theatre.

'Is Rose doing it too?' Jessie asked.

I nodded and took a sip of juice. Rose is my best friend and we go to school together. We also go to ballet lessons every week at Miss Nancy's dancing school.

'We've been practising for ages,' I told Jessie, 'but there's so much to remember!'

'I bet,' said Jessie.

Jessie was drinking a big mug of tea. Jessie is famous in the Grand Theatre for her cups of tea.

'Do you have to do a dance for your exam?' Jessie asked.

'Yes,' I said, putting down my cup and springing up from my stool. 'It's really cool.'

I twirled around and showed her some of the steps, finishing in a little curtsey.

'Meowwwww!'

Jessie and I giggled. Giselle, the theatre cat, stood up from her basket, looked at me, and purred.

'I think Giselle likes your dance!' said Jessie.

And we both laughed again.

We had found Giselle and her kittens hiding in the theatre not so long ago. Now she lives there and everyone loves her. We called her Giselle because she is white and beautiful and everyone thought she was a ghost, just like the character in the ballet *Giselle*.

'We still haven't learned all the steps,' I explained to Jessie as I stroked Giselle. 'Hey – I've just remembered something!'

I raced over to my school bag and pulled out a picture that I'd drawn.

'Here!' I handed it to Jessie.

9

'It's gorgeous!' Jessie declared. 'Look, Giselle, Tilly's drawn a picture of Myrtha! I'll put it on the wall.'

Myrtha's my cat, and one of Giselle's kittens. Like her mum, she's got lots of white fur but instead of being white all over, she's got little black toes that look like she's wearing pointe shoes.

'But it will have to wait till later,' said Jessie. 'Now you must get down to the studio for Extras.'

Extras is a special ballet class that I go to every Saturday with Rose. It's brilliant. We get taught by the same teachers as the dancers of the Grand Ballet and we dance in the same studios they use!

I gave Giselle a gentle stroke and picked up my ballet bag.

'I've got to take some things to the shoe room so I'll come some of the way with you,' said Jessie, picking up a big box.

'What's in there?' I asked.

Jessie always has packages full of interesting things, like silky fabrics, pretty ribbons and silvery sequins.

'Crystals,' said Jessie. 'We're going to put them on the costumes and shoes in *Cinderella*.'

'Wow!' I sighed, following Jessie down the corridor.

Cinderella is the new ballet they're about to put on. My mum is playing Cinderella. And my dad is the prince! They've been rehearsing for months and everything is almost ready for the opening night next Saturday. They're just carrying out the finishing touches.

'Look!' I stopped in my tracks. There was a poster for *Cinderella* on one of the notice boards. It showed my mum and dad.

I stood, gazing at the sumptuous ball gown my mum was wearing.

I think it's cool that Mum and Dad are dancers with the Grand Ballet. Even if it means I don't get to see them that much because they're always at the theatre. And it's the reason I love dancing.

'Tilly,' Jessie said, anxiously, 'look at the time!' She pointed at the clock on the wall. 'If you don't hurry up, you'll miss the start of your class!'

There was five minutes, and I still had to put my shoes on! I've never run so fast in my life!

Chapter Two

I dashed down the corridor and into the changing room. Rose was already there, dressed and ready.

'I thought you weren't coming!' she exclaimed.

'Nearly done,' I gasped, hastily pulling on the pink crossover cardigan my gran had made. It was only six weeks until Christmas and I was glad to have the crossover – it was getting cold!

'Hey – who's that?' I hissed, nodding

13

towards the older girls who were already on their way out of the changing room.

Veronica was one of them. She always acts like she's in charge. And she doesn't like us younger kids. Today, there was someone new with her.

'I don't know,' said Rose. 'But it looks like she's Veronica's friend – let's go!'

I pulled on my shoes, then Rose and I raced into the studio. We arrived at the *barre* just as Miss Marion opened the door for our class to begin!

Miss Marion is our teacher and she's great. Extras isn't like a regular ballet class. We do *barre* work and centre work, of course, but we don't follow a set programme. Each week, Miss Marion gives us a new routine to learn. It keeps us on our toes. Or, as my dad says, my Tilly Tiptoes!

We took out places at the *barre*. Miss

Marion likes the younger girls at the front and the taller ones at the back. This always makes Veronica cross because she likes to be at the front, where Miss Marion can see her. Veronica is good, but she thinks she's brilliant and she's not – she's still learning like the rest of us. My dad says that even professional dancers learn something new every day.

Before the class started, Miss Marion made an announcement.

'Morning, everyone,' she said. 'I'd like to introduce you to Karina.'

She beckoned the new girl to the front of the studio. The girl smiled and looked around the room, blushing a bit.

'Karina has just moved here and we're very pleased that she'll be joining us. I'm sure you'll all make her welcome. Now,' Miss Marion turned to look along the *barre*, 'where shall we put you?'

'Please, Miss Marion!' Veronica was waving her hand in the air. 'There's a space free here!'

She moved back so that the girl behind her on the *barre* had to move too.

'Excellent,' said Miss Marion as Karina slipped into place. 'Everyone ready? Let's begin.'

Because the studio had mirrors all around it, Rose and I caught glimpses of Karina as we did our *pliés*, our *ronde de jambe*, and then our *grand battement*.

Karina was good. She could get her legs really high in *arabesque*. And we could see Veronica trying to make sure she was getting hers just as high. Her face was red with the effort.

When we moved to the centre, Miss Marion gave us all different variations of the same routine so the younger dancers, like Rose and me, could do less strenuous versions of the steps. I tried to remember to smile, as Miss Nancy, my other teacher, always tells us to do. And I tried to keep my balance when I lifted my legs *en l'air*.

After our *reverence* at the end of the lesson, Rose and I skipped back to the changing room.

'Hello,' I said to Karina.

'You were really good,' sighed Rose.

'Thanks,' said Karina.

But before she could say any more, Veronica grabbed the new girl's arm, and swept her away.

'Oh, you don't want to talk to those dweebs,' she hissed. 'They're just a pain!'

'Really!' said Rose.

'I know,' I agreed. 'But how unlucky for Karina – it looks like Veronica wants to be her friend!'

And Rose and I burst into giggles.

From the other side of the changing room, Veronica gave us her fiercest glare. Which made us giggle even more!

Chapter Three

Mum and Dad came to collect me from the ballet wardrobe after their rehearsal. I love it when they don't have any performances on Saturday because it means I get them all to myself!

When we got home, I started to practise my dance.

One, two, three . . . two, two, three . . . three, two, three . . . I counted in my head as I skipped, pointed and twirled.

My dance tells a story. Miss Nancy

explained that we are in a garden, reading, when suddenly we hear a bird singing. So we start to look for the bird and find it perched in a tree. Then we dance around the garden with the bird fluttering about with us. Occasionally the bird lands on our shoulder and, at the end, it is sitting on our finger while we finish by pointing our right foot out in front of us. It's a really sweet dance. And the music sounds just like a bird singing!

Anyway, I was dancing happily and it was going really well. I was at the part when the bird is on my shoulder when suddenly my mind went completely blank. I couldn't remember what steps came next! I hesitated for a moment, going over the last steps again. I carried on with the next few movements but then I realised I was travelling in the wrong direction. Whoops!

'That's looking good,' said Mum, coming into the room.

'But I've just gone wrong,' I replied and explained the problem.

'Why not start again from the beginning?' Mum suggested.

It did help. I got further than before. But then I went the wrong way again.

'If I can't even do this bit, how am I going to remember the whole dance when it comes to the exam?' I complained.

'The best thing is to practise,' said Mum. 'Practise, practise, practise. That's all a dancer can do. The more you do it, the better you'll get. It's just like when Dad plays the piano!'

'What's this about me and the piano?' said Dad, appearing at the door.

I told him the trouble I was having learning my dance.

'Hmmm,' Dad agreed. 'What Mum says is true ... You just have to keep practising and then one day you'll suddenly get it! I have the same problem learning my steps. I keep getting things wrong in rehearsals, don't I, Susanna?'

Mum nodded. 'Always! And then, just before the performance it's like a switch goes "click" in your head and everything goes smoothly in the end.'

Dad gave me a hug. 'Sorry, Tilly – it sounds like you're just like your dad.'

I felt loads better after hearing that.

'Now,' said Mum, 'I fancy some hot chocolate with a swirl of cream on top! Would you like some too?'

'Yes, please!' Dad and I said at the same time.

It got dark really early that afternoon so I snuggled up with *The Great Big Book of Ballet Stories* on the sofa. Myrtha was sleeping next to me and I was lost in the tale of *Cinderella* when Dad came into the room.

'Hey, Tilly,' he said. 'Recognise this?'

He sat down at the piano and started playing. It was the music for my dance!

I leapt up and started dancing along.

'How did you know what to play?'

'Ah!' said Dad, quickly lifting his right hand from the keys and tapping his nose knowingly. 'A little bird told me . . . Now, come on – let's start from the beginning.'

I ran to the corner of the room and got into position, arms *en courant*, my right foot pointed behind me. *Pull up through the top of your head, shoulders down, knees turned out*, I heard Miss Nancy say.

'I'll be the audience,' said Dad. 'Let the music help you to remember the steps. Now – are you ready?'

'OK!' I smiled.

Dad played the opening chords and off I set. *Glissades*, gallops, *jetés*, *chassés*, step and point. The steps were easier to remember when I listened to the music, although I did get a bit confused at one point about which leg to use and I made some other small mistakes. Still, I got all the way through the dance.

'Well that seemed to go OK,' said Dad, smiling.

'Thanks,' I nodded. The music had made a big difference. But I still needed to get it perfect . . .

'Can we do it again?' I asked.

'Of course,' said Dad. 'Overture and beginners on stage!'

Chapter Four

Mum came to meet me after school on Monday.

'Come on,' she said. 'I need to pick up a few bits and pieces. Would you like to buy some new ballet shoes for your exam!'

'Yes, please!' I grinned.

We went to *Dance! Dance!* It's the best shop ever. For my ballet lessons, I wear pink leather ballet shoes. But for exams I have shiny, pink satin ones.

I tried on two or three different pairs

until we found some that were just the right fit. Mum always says it's really important that the shoes fit properly. Too tight and they will hurt, but too big and you won't be able to point your toes perfectly.

'And we'll take some ribbon to match,' Mum said to Mrs Grace, the lady who owns the shop.

With my leather shoes, I have elastic to keep them on. But with the satin ones, Mum sews on ribbons and then I wrap them around my ankle.

'There you are, Chantilly,' said Mrs Grace, handing me a bag with my beatiful shoes and ribbons inside. 'And good luck!'

Back home, Mum sat down with a cup of hot chocolate and her huge bag of ballet stuff, plus my bag of new shoes.

Myrtha, who is nosy like Giselle, jumped onto the sofa and poked her nose into the bag. I giggled and stroked her as she settled on my lap.

'I thought we should sew on the ribbons,' said Mum as she took out the spool of pink ribbon.

Myrtha and I watched as she cut four pieces of the same length and put them to one side.

'How do you know where to place the ribbons?' I asked.

'Well every dancer is slightly different,' Mum explained. 'But you fold the back of the shoe over onto the inner lining and, usually, you attach the ribbons just in front of where the back of the shoe folds. I'll pin this one and then you can try it before I stitch it in place.'

I gently placed Myrtha on the sofa and put on the shoe. Mum bent down and took the inside ribbon and wrapped it around my ankle, bringing it to rest on the inside just where the knobbly bone is. Then she took the outer ribbon and did the same thing. She tied a knot and tucked the ends into the wrapped ribbon.

'Point your toe for me?' Mum suggested. So I did.

'Well the ribbon's not gaping so that's about right!' Mum said. 'Let's do the same with the other shoe and then I can fasten them on.'

'Why don't ribbons get tied in bows on the outside of the foot?' I asked as Mum sewed.

'You don't want people in the audience admiring your bows, do you?' Mum said. 'The idea is that they should see your beautiful pointing feet and not even notice the shoes, let alone the ribbons!'

I'd have to remember that the next time I did up the shoes on my own!

With the ribbons securely sewn in, Mum took a pen and wrote my name in neat, tiny writing on the soles of my shoes.

'If you point your toes properly, no one

should be able to read that,' she said. 'And if you forget your shoes in the changing room, everyone will know they are yours! Here, you fold that one and I'll do this one.'

Together, we folded each shoe, backs down first like before, then the inner side into the middle, followed by the outer side. Now the shoes were small and flat, we took the ribbons and wrapped them neatly around the ends.

'Pop them in your bag so we know they'll be there,' said Mum. 'With the ribbons wrapped like that, they won't get knotty and tangled.'

After doing my shoes, Mum spent the rest of the afternoon sewing ribbons and elastic on her own new shoes. We chatted about *Cinderella* while she worked.

'Just wait till you see Snowdrop,' Mum said.

'Snowdrop?' I asked, puzzled. 'Who's that?'

'A pony!' Mum smiled.

'A pony? In a ballet?' I wondered.

Mum nodded. 'She pulls Cinderella's coach to the ball.'

'No way!' I exclaimed. 'It's going to be the best show ever!'

Chapter Five

The next day, Rose's mum Helen took us to Miss Nancy's and I told them about Snowdrop on the way.

'A real pony?' Rose gasped. 'How amazing!'

'I know,' I said. 'Mum says she wears a sparkly harness and everything.'

'I can't wait to see her,' said Rose as Helen opened the door to the hall.

But we didn't get a chance to talk any more about Snowdrop. Helen had spotted a notice on the wall.

'Look!' she said. 'Your exam date has been confirmed. It's not this Saturday but the next.'

'I feel sick,' I said to Rose.

'Me too,' she replied. 'But if we do everything Miss Nancy has taught us, we should be OK, shouldn't we?'

I looked at my best friend and hugged her. 'Course we will. Come on – let's go and get ready.'

To keep my new shoes looking nice, I wore my old leather ones for class. We went through all the exercises that we'd been practising.

'Don't forget to smile at the examiner, girls!' Miss Nancy said as we did our centre work.

'Eyes up, ladies,' she said later as we did our *port de bras*.

Then it was time to do our dance. With Miss Nancy's permission, I changed into my new shoes. Mum had said it would be a good idea to wear them for the dance, so I could start to mould them to my feet. Some of the other girls did the same.

'Now I'm going to teach you the last part of the dance,' Miss Nancy said as we gathered back in the studio. 'Let's listen to the music first . . .'

We heard the notes of the final section play and watched as Miss Nancy showed us the steps that went with it.

'Now, girls, you try!' Miss Nancy said, turning to face us.

One, two, three . . . two, two, three . . . three, two, three . . . and off we set. On its own, the sequence of steps wasn't that hard. The dance finished with us pointing our toe out in front, *en diagonale*, holding the bird perched on our finger and our other hand out pointing towards it.

'Right, girls,' Miss Nancy said as the music stopped. 'Shall we do it all the way through from the beginning?'

Oh no! I thought. *Will I be able to remember everything?*

Let the music help you, I heard Dad saying inside my head. I listened to him – and the music – when the pianist started again.

But I set off on the wrong leg. And then I forgot what came next. Rose got it right though. So did Sophie, Chloe and most of the class. I felt awful.

'Let's try that again,' Miss Nancy smiled.

She didn't say anything about me being hopeless.

We repeated the dance. And this time I got all the steps right. Well, almost . . .

'Much better, girls,' said Miss Nancy.

'Now make sure you practise your dance at home. And don't forget to take these letters when you leave. Time for your *reverence*!'

We curtsied, just like we would for the examiner, and then stood in a line in front of Miss Nancy, ready to take our letters.

'Give these to your parents,' Miss Nancy said. 'They have the details of your exam.'

I tucked the note in my ballet bag and then quickly got changed. Slipping into my thick winter coat and shoes, I caught sight of one of the photographs on the wall. It was Mum when she was my age and one of Miss Nancy's pupils. She looked so beautiful and confident. I wondered if she had been nervous about taking her ballet exams too?

Chapter Six

After class, Rose's mum took me to the Grand Theatre. I was glad to get into the warm. It was freezing outside!

'Evening, Tilly!' said Bob, the man who sits at the Stage Door. He was surrounded by a pile of boxes.

'Hi, Bob. What are you doing?' I asked.

'I'm trying to check these delivery lists. Only most of my paperwork is underneath this large paperweight . . .' Bob pointed to the purring bundle of fur on his desk.

Giselle tweaked her ear and, very slowly, opened one eye. She purred louder as I leaned forward and gave her a stroke.

'Hey, Giselle,' I whispered. 'You look cosy there.'

'Are you off to see Jessie?' Bob asked.

I nodded. And, at the sound of Jessie's name, Giselle stood up and began to stretch.

'Tell her to put the kettle on, will you?' said Bob. 'I'll be along in a minute for a cup of tea.'

'Of course,' I said, setting off towards the ballet wardrobe. Giselle, who had finished stretching, jumped off Bob's desk and followed me.

'Hi, Tilly!' said a group of dancers, who were standing reading some of the notice boards that lined the corridor. Mia and Gus, two former Extras pupils, were among them.

'Hello!' I called back.

I love walking around the Grand Theatre. There is always someone who knows you and will stop to chat. It's like being part of one great big family!

When we got to the big red swing doors of the ballet wardrobe, Giselle rushed ahead of me and stood there purring. I think she was hungry.

'Hello?' I called as I pushed open the door.

'Tilly!' said Jessie. She was sitting at her worktable with the rest of the wardrobe team. Belinda and Adam help Jessie to make the costumes. And Mary and Amber are dressers – they help the dancers put on their costumes and headdresses.

Giselle made straight for her bowl of water and started to drink.

'Welcome back, Giselle,' smiled Belinda.

'She was asleep on Bob's desk when I arrived,' I told them. And everyone giggled and said how much Giselle enjoyed nosing around the theatre.

Jessie's worktable was covered in lists and at the side of the room there were rails hanging with gorgeous glittering costumes.

'We're just going through who is wearing what in *Cinderella*,' Jessie explained. 'We won't be long and then we'll stop for tea!'

'Oh good,' I said. 'That reminds me – Bob said he'd pop by for a cup soon. While you finish, shall I go on a pin hunt?'

'Yes, please!' said Jessie.

I fished out Jessie's special horseshoe-shaped magnet from her workbasket. Looking for pins and needles that have dropped on the floor is one of the jobs I always help Jessie with. I love the way they all jump onto the magnet as I wave it around.

'So what have you been doing today?' Jessie asked later, when she was finished.

I told her all about my ballet class and wearing my new shoes.

'I'm having problems remembering all the steps for my dance though.'

'Don't worry – you will in the end.'

'That's what everyone says,' I sighed.

Just then, Bob appeared and he chatted with everyone as they sipped their tea. Behind the rails of costumes, I went through my dance. *Jeté*, *glissade* and *chassé*. Yes! I had finished on the right leg! I did it a couple more times then Jessie called out:

'Hey, Tilly? Where are you?'

I popped my head out from the costumes.

'Ah!' she smiled. 'Would you like to come with me to see Harry?'

'Harry?' I asked. 'What for?'

Harry is the property master and he's in charge of all the props they use on stage. Things like boxes and baskets, and the wands that the dancers use to help tell their stories.

'Well, Cinderella's coach has been finished,' Jessie explained. 'But Harry needs a hand securing the door catches and he wondered if I could help.'

'Cinderella's coach?' I shrieked. 'Let's go!'

Chapter Seven

The coach was magical! And much bigger than I'd imagined but, as Harry explained, Cinderella did have to sit in it. And once it was on stage it would look much smaller.

'Fancy a seat, Tilly?' Harry asked, opening the shimmering gold door.

'Can I?' I gasped. 'It's so beautiful!'

'Course you can!' said Harry. 'You too, Jessie, if you like. You can look at the problem with the door catch while you're there.'

I watched as Jessie did some stitching on the catch to make the door close firmly from the inside.

'Finished,' Jessie said, putting her things away. Then she waved her hand through the window. 'I feel like a queen!'

'I feel like a princess!' I said, waving too.

'So will it do to carry Cinderella to the ball?' Harry wondered.

'It's absolutely perfect!' I nodded. 'And I'm dying to see what Snowdrop looks like in front of it!'

'Well the best we can offer is some of the designer's drawings,' suggested Jessie. 'Shall we go back to the wardrobe and take a look?'

I nodded enthusiastically. I couldn't wait!

Back in the ballet wardrobe, Giselle was fast asleep in her basket.

'Honestly,' said Jessie, as she rummaged in a cupboard. 'When she isn't on a tour of the theatre, all she does is sleep.'

'Or eat!' I giggled. 'Myrtha is just the same.'

'Got them,' said Jessie, pulling out a folder from her cupboard. 'Here . . .'

She placed the drawings on the worktable.

'Oh look!' I gasped.

A sweet little white pony with glittering feathery plumes on its head was pulling Cinderella's coach.

'Snowdrop's going to look fantastic!' I exclaimed.

I couldn't resist peeking at the other drawings the designer had done. One showed Cinderella in her rag dress, sweeping the floor in the kitchen. One revealed her transformation into a beautiful dancer at the ball. And of course there was one of her wedding gown. Others showed Buttons, Prince Charming, and the Ugly Sisters.

As I gazed at the costume designs, I got lost in the music that was playing through the theatre's loud speakers, imagining I was Cinderella in her ragged dress. I don't know how long I stood there, thinking about the steps and swooning to the music. Suddenly I felt a tap on my shoulder and jumped.

'Sorry, Tilly!'

It was Dad! And Mum was behind him.

'How did your ballet class go today?' she asked. 'Did you remember the steps of your dance?'

I nodded. 'Sort of . . . Miss Nancy gave me this letter for you – it's about the exam!' I said, taking it from my ballet bag.

Mum read it quickly.

'I don't believe it!' she said. 'Your exam is on the same day as the Gala show!'

'We won't be able to come with you,' said Dad. 'We'll be rehearsing. Helen will have to take you. Or maybe Gran?'

I bit my lip. Why could Mum and Dad never be with me for important things?

Sometimes it seemed really unfair! I'd feel much more confident about remembering my dance steps if they were there.

I tried to hide my disappointment.

'What's a Gala show?' was all I managed to say.

'It's a very special performance of a ballet,' Mum said. 'It'll be a week after the opening night on Saturday. There's a guest of honour and all the audience dress up. Sometimes the Gala raises money for charity from the ticket sales.'

'I heard Madame Satina is going to be the special guest!' Jessie said.

Madame Satina was the founder of the Grand Ballet.

'And the good news is that I've bought tickets for you to come to the Gala with Gran and Helen and Rose,' Mum announced.

'Wow!' I sighed. 'Thanks.' I'd seen photographs of Madame Satina talking to my mum and dad. She was quite an old lady but she still had a ballerina's straight back and turned-out feet. It would be really special to see Madame Satina as well as a performance of *Cinderella*.

Mum gave me a big hug.

'I'm sorry about your exam, Tilly. But I hope going to the Gala show will make up for it a little,' she said.

I tried to smile but I wasn't happy. I mean, the Gala would be great, but it wasn't the same as having Mum and Dad come to wish me luck as I went into my exam . . .

Chapter Eight

On Thursday, it rained all day. We weren't
allowed out at break to play or anything.
But Rose and I did lots of drawing and
colouring instead. I did a picture of
Cinderella's coach and I tried hard to
remember exactly what Harry's one had
looked like.

After school, I took the picture with me
to the theatre.

'I drew this for Harry,' I said, showing it
to Jessie.

'That's splendid,' Jessie said. 'He'll love it. We'll take it to him in a minute. On our way to deliver these.'

Jessie was putting piles of boxes into a huge basket on wheels. She used it to take things around the theatre.

'What's in there?' I wanted to know.

'Bits and pieces for the shoe master and the wig master,' Jessie explained. 'Shall we go?'

As if she understood every word, Giselle stood up from the worktable, where she'd been curled up asleep, and with great elegance jumped into the basket.

Jessie and I laughed.

'Looks like Giselle's coming too!' I said.

We went to see Harry first and gave him my picture. He thanked me and stuck it on the wall next to his worktable. Then we pushed the basket along the corridor until we came to the shoe room. Jessie knocked on the big blue door.

'Anyone at home?' she asked, pushing open the door and peeking inside.

'Hello, Jessie!'

It was Gerda, the shoe master. She looks after all the ballet shoes at the theatre.

The shoe room is incredible. It has every type of dancing shoe. Shelves and shelves of them almost from floor to ceiling. Each shelf had a label with the shoe size, type of shoe and its colour. Other shelves had labels with the names of dancers on them and were filled with a mixture of shoes.

'Are those more crystals?' Gerda asked as Jessie started to unload some boxes from the basket.

Jessie nodded.

'What are you going to do with them?' I asked.

'I'm going to put them on some of the shoes in the ball scene in *Cinderella*,' Gerda explained. 'Here – I'll show you the designs.'

Just like Jessie, Gerda also had a worktable. It was covered in all sorts of tools, sewing kit, fabric paints and paintbrushes. On one side of the table, Gerda had sketches of the designs, and on the other was a pair of shoes that she was working on.

They looked like the ones people wore in fairy tales. They were made of satin that had been dyed a gorgeous deep pink – a bit like raspberries. And on top of the satin, was a sprinkling of crystals.

'What do you think, Tilly?' Gerda asked, holding up the shoe to the light.

It was like a rainbow was bursting out of each crystal.

'They're beautiful!' I sighed.

'Glad you like them,' Gerda grinned.

'And thanks for my boxes, Jessie!'

'You're welcome,' said Jessie. She looked at her watch. 'But we'd better get going now. We've got more to deliver.'

Our next stop was the wig master's room. Just like the shoe room, the walls were lined with shelves. But instead of being able to see what was on them, this time they were full of big brown cardboard boxes.

Maurice the wig master greeted us when we arrived.

Maurice is in charge of all the wigs and hairpieces that are worn. In some ballets, the dancers have their hair in a bun or hanging loose. But at other times they have to wear wigs.

'Look at that!' I said, walking over to the worktable. On top of a model head, there was a wig made of different shades of lavender and purple. It looked like the hair had been spun like spiders' webs and twirled like cream into a whipped creation piled higher and higher to a point at the top.

'Who's going to wear that?' I asked.

'It's for one of the Ugly Sisters,' Maurice smiled. 'I'm going to put some crystals on it to make it even more elaborate.

'Speaking of which . . .' said Jessie. And she took some boxes out of her basket.

'Excellent,' Maurice said. 'Just in time!'

'Can I come back and see it when it's finished?' I asked.

'Of course,' said Maurice. He picked up a long piece of purple hair and started to form it into another curl.

It's like everything at the Grand Theatre is magic.

Chapter Nine

On Saturday, as we changed for our Extras class, I told Rose all about the shoes and wigs. We were still busy chatting as we headed for the studio.

'Excuse me!' Veronica barged past, as she marched down the corridor.

'Whoa!' Rose and I said as we were pushed out of the way.

Karina, who was with her, stopped dead in her tracks, her mouth open.

'Hey! What gives you the right . . .'

But Veronica just turned round and gave us one of her nasty looks. Then she grabbed Karina by the arm.

'Take no notice of those two,' she said. 'They're just stupid.'

'They look OK to me,' Karina said, pulling her arm away. 'See you in class.' Then she turned on her heels and walked away.

'Karina! Wait!' cried Veronica, her face flushed and she raced to catch up with her.

Rose and I giggled as we carried on walking.

'Looks like Karina has got Veronica sussed,' Rose said.

'Yes,' I replied. 'But you can be sure Veronica's not going to give up on her that easily.'

Rose agreed. Veronica always latched onto the best dancers at Extras. And from what we'd seen so far, Karina was something special.

'You two OK?' someone behind us asked.

It was Rupert, one of the older boys.

'Don't worry about Veronica – she's just plain rude,' he said.

We nodded and, entering the studio, took our normal places at the *barre*.

I could see Veronica's reflection in the mirror. She was at the other end of the *barre*. She caught my eye and gave another sneer. I waved back and smiled my sweetest smile. You should have seen her expression!

But before she could do anything else, Miss Marion swept into the studio, clapped her hands and the class began. When we got to the centre work, we took it in turns to dance in our lines so we saw more of Karina dancing. She was really good!

I mean, proper amazing. She jumped like she had springs in her feet. She could even do pirouettes without wobbling. I couldn't imagine ever being that good. As I watched Karina dance, I bet she didn't have any problems with her ballet exams. I bet she always remembered her steps . . .

When the class was over, I tried to speak to Karina in the changing room. But Veronica just butted in over the top of me so I gave up.

'Oh, Karina! How did you learn to spot like that?' she crooned.

I don't know what Karina said, but she didn't stay for long, even though Veronica tried to make her keep talking. The new girl simply pulled on her tracksuit over her ballet clothes and slipped her feet out of her ballet shoes and into some trainers.

'Bye, everyone,' she said, catching me and Rose with a smile as she left.

'Bye!' we all said.

And Vile Veronica was left in the changing room. All on her bossy own!

Chapter Ten

There was a matinee and an evening performance of *Cinderella* that day. The first performances of the ballet's season. I was desperate to see the show but it would be special to wait until Gala night. Anyway, Gran had come to look after me for the weekend. Gran is my mum's mum and she's the best gran ever. She was waiting at home when Helen dropped me off.

'Hello, Tilly darling!' she said, opening the door.

I raced over and gave her a hug.

'Gosh it's chilly, isn't it!' said Gran, rubbing her hands. 'Quick – let's get into the warm!'

Myrtha came rushing up to say hello, then she followed us upstairs. I showed Gran the brilliant poster on my bedroom wall – it was something Dad gave me. I'm the ballerina on the poster, as if I'm the star of the ballet!

'Isn't that wonderful!' Gran said. She scooped Myrtha into her arms. 'Maybe one day you'll be the ballerina in a ballet. I can remember when your mum had dreams just like you. And look at her now! And look at you, Myrtha, wearing your own ballet shoes!'

'Did Mum do ballet exams when she was a girl?' I asked Gran when we sat down to eat lunch.

'She certainly did,' said Gran. 'Just like you. But it wasn't always easy for her.'

'Really?' I was amazed. My mum is a brilliant dancer and I'd always thought she must have been like that.

'Yes,' Gran carried on. 'I remember one exam when she came down with chicken pox two weeks before!'

'What happened?' I gasped.

'Luckily, she got better just in time,' smiled Gran.

'And did she pass?'

Gran nodded. 'She got Honours. We were so proud.'

'Did Mum always love ballet?' I wondered.

'Yes,' said Gran, thoughtfully. 'Though she didn't want to go to lessons at first . . .'

'Why not?'

'She was nervous,' Gran explained. 'She

kept saying "I won't know what to do!" and "I won't know anyone!" But at the end of her first class she didn't want to leave!'

I laughed and remembered that I'd felt the same way.

'Your mum came home from that lesson and did the exercises over and over again,' Gran carried on. 'I had to force her to go to bed. But then she'd be practising again as soon as she got up! She never stopped.'

'That's why she's so good now,' I said, proudly. Maybe if I kept practising, I'd be that good too.

'Just like you will be,' said Gran, as if she could read my thoughts. 'Now, eat up. I've got a surprise for us!'

Gran is good at surprises! She wouldn't give me any clues. Not even when we got on the bus. The bus trundled along, past all the shops with their Christmassy windows. I had no idea where we were going, but we got off outside a museum.

'Are we going inside?' I asked.

Gran nodded. 'It has some things I thought you'd like to see . . .'

We walked along the marble-lined corridors, glancing at all kinds of beautiful paintings and statues and objects in glass cabinets.

'Here,' said Gran, gently pulling me through a door.

'Wow!' I gasped.

The sign said 'Welcome to the Theatre Galleries' and the place was full of costumes, scenery, props, photographs, shoes . . . Some items were from operas, others from plays and musicals. And there was a whole section just about ballet.

'This is amazing!' I said. 'Look at that tutu!' It was black and gold and just spectacular.

'I thought you'd like it here,' Gran smiled. 'Come on – let's explore.'

Gran and I looked at the costumes. We even found one that had been worn by my dad. It was from *Peter and the Wolf* and Dad had been the wolf.

Gran and I giggled as we thought about how we'd dance in some of the costumes. I fell in love with an absolutely stunning outfit for a fairy. It was a long floaty dress with pieces of silky blue-and-silver material that kind of wafted around. There was a photo of the dancer in it and you could see that as she moved the dress swirled up around her like it was floating. I wanted to wear that dress!

Gran's favourite was an orange and red tutu from *The Firebird*. It was all spiky and firey – just like the character who would wear it. I could have stayed there for hours. The only reason we left was because the museum was closing and we were asked to go home.

Chapter Eleven

After school on Tuesday, Helen took me and Rose to Miss Nancy's. This was our last class before our exam. But on Friday we were going to have an extra lesson – an exam rehearsal.

Miss Nancy worked us hard.

'Straighten your knees!' she shouted as we did our *ronde de jambes*.

'Pull up from your hips!' she reminded us when we did our *port de bras*.

'Breathe through your noses,' she said.

'We don't want to catch flies in our mouths, do we?'

I wanted to laugh when she said that and could feel my mouth curling up at the edges. But somehow I think Miss Nancy knew and, before I could, she said:

'Smile nicely, Tilly – that's it. It makes you look like you're enjoying yourself. And if you're enjoying yourself, the examiner might as well!'

And then I got to the bit I was dreading. Our dance. I had butterflies in my tummy as we went to the top corner of the studio to begin. Would I remember it . . . ?

'Keep smiling, girls!' Miss Nancy encouraged.

But as the opening chords of the music began, I couldn't smile *and* try to remember the steps. I skipped, galloped, *jetéd*, pointed, and jumped. I had no time to wonder how far into the dance I'd got. All I wanted to do was the next step, then the next, and the next. Only I didn't get to the final bit. The bit we'd learnt recently. I was thinking so hard I didn't look where I was going. Next thing, I was on the wrong foot and all the others were suddenly next to me. Whoops! I tripped. Worse! I bumped into the others. The whole dance ended.

'Oh dear,' said Miss Nancy, her eyebrows raised.

My cheeks were burning. I felt such an idiot.

'Let's run through that bit again, shall we?' Miss Nancy said, kindly.

My brain went blank. I couldn't remember any of the steps. So when we began again, I concentrated hard on what Rose and the other girls were doing. It was more like marking than dancing.

But I got to the end that time. And I didn't bump into anyone.

'Much better, girls,' said Miss Nancy.

Then, after our *reverence*, Miss Nancy came over to me as we were leaving.

Please don't let her tell me that I'm not good enough to take the exam, I thought.

'Don't worry about the dance, Tilly,' she said, putting her hand on my shoulder. 'It'll be fine. But perhaps you should practise at home – just to go over the steps? Then you'll find it easier on Friday.'

Friday? In only four days time it will be the actual exam, I thought.

I nodded, grateful that I was still doing the exam. But my eyes were prickling with tears. I gulped. I really didn't want to cry in front of everyone . . .

'How was the dance today?' Jessie asked when Helen had dropped me off at the theatre.

I sat stroking Giselle as I told Jessie all about it. Big, fat, blobby tears began to pour down my face.

'Don't worry.' Jessie hugged me. 'Your dad never remembers his steps until the first performance.'

I buried my head in Jessie's neck. Giselle rubbed her face on my arm as if to hug me too.

'But my exam is on Saturday!' I wailed.

'Come on,' said Adam and Belinda, who were at the worktable, making some last-minute adjustments to the costumes. 'Why don't you try it again now? We'll help.'

They cleared away the chairs and Adam placed Giselle on the worktable where she sat and licked her paws.

'It's a bit cramped,' said Belinda. 'But let's see how you do.'

I blew my nose, wiped my eyes, and went over to the corner, imagining the music playing in my head. I counted myself in as Belinda, Adam, and Jessie sat at the front of my impromptu 'studio'. Then I began to dance. And this time I didn't put a foot wrong! Perhaps at last everything had begun to 'click', just like Dad – and Jessie – said it would.

'Bravo!' everyone clapped and cheered when I finished.

'Let's celebrate with a nice cup of tea,' said Jessie.

But before she could put the kettle on, the door swung open and a lady that I didn't recognise came in.

'Good evening, Antonia,' Jessie smiled. 'What can we do for you? And have you met Tilly, my goddaughter?'

'Hello, Tilly,' Antonia said. 'Actually, it was you I've come to see.'

Me? Why? I wondered.

'You know it's our Gala show on Saturday?' Antonia said.

I nodded.

'And you know that the guest of honour is Madame Satina?' Antonia added.

'Oh yes,' said Jessie. 'It's very exciting.'

'Well, I need someone to present a bouquet of flowers to Madame Satina when she arrives,' Antonia said, looking at me. 'And I wondered if you'd like to do that?'

I felt a rush of excitement.

'Me? Present a bouquet? At the Gala?' I gasped. 'Yes, please!'

Jessie clapped her hands. She was just as excited as I was.

'You'll need to wear a beautiful dress!' said Adam.

'Do you have a party dress?' asked Belinda.

'I do!' I said. 'But it might be a bit small now . . .'

I'd had it since last Christmas and I knew I'd grown taller since then.

'Oh,' said Jessie. 'I think a special occasion like this calls for a special dress, don't you?'

'But there's no time to buy a new one,' I said. 'Mum and Dad have got performances most of the week.'

'May I remind you, Tilly Tiptoes, that you are in the wardrobe of the Grand Theatre – I think that Adam, Belinda and myself are more than qualified to make you a special dress!'

'You'll make me my own dress?' I gasped.

'What colour?' asked Belinda.

'What fabric?' wondered Adam.

'Hmmm,' said Jessie. 'How about we get some materials sorted and have them ready for tomorrow? Then we can do a fitting and get stitching straightaway.'

Chapter Twelve

'No way!' screamed Rose when I told her the next day. 'You get to meet Madame Satina *and* wear a beautiful new dress! You're so lucky!'

'I know,' I said. 'I'm going to choose the material when I go to the theatre this evening!'

'There's so much going on,' said Rose. 'I can't wait till the Gala show.'

'Yes,' I agreed. 'But first we've got to get through our ballet exam . . .'

I was feeling better about my dance after Jessie's help the night before. And I'd done some more practising when I got home too. I really *really* wanted to get it right in the exam rehearsal on Friday.

It was hard to concentrate at school that day. I was glad when the bell went for the end of the afternoon. And I was even gladder when Dad came to meet me and took me to the theatre. There wasn't a performance that night but they were having lighting and sound checks on stage, so Dad had to go along for a bit.

'I'll see you later,' Dad said, rubbing his hands to get warm as he dropped me off at the ballet wardrobe.

'Knock, knock!' I opened the door.

'Hello, Tilly!' everyone greeted me.

Jessie, Belinda and Adam were there along with Amber and Mary.

'Hello! Where's Giselle?' I asked, taking off my winter coat and looking around the room. She wasn't in her basket having her usual afternoon nap.

'Off exploring, I expect,' said Jessie. 'She's always out and about right now.'

'She's on a big adventure today,' said Belinda. 'I haven't seen her since lunch.'

'She'll be back when she's hungry,' laughed Adam.

'We've been thinking about your special dress,' Jessie said.

'I haven't *stopped* thinking about it!' I exclaimed.

Jessie laughed. 'I've done some sketches – here.' She pushed some pieces of paper across the worktable towards me. 'What do you think?'

There were five different designs, each one with a little girl who looked ever so similar to me. They were all gorgeous, but one of them jumped out straightaway.

'This one,' I sighed. 'I love it!'

The picture showed a fitted bodice with a sash around the high waist. And then the skirt fell away in floating sections. It was like the costume I'd fallen in love with at the museum!

'Good choice!' everyone agreed.

'What sort of colours?' Jessie asked.

Jessie and Adam held up big rolls of fabric and let some of the shimmering sheer silks hang down and catch the light.

'I like that one! And that!' I said, pointing to different tones of blue and purple.

'Gerda's going to come along to see what you've chosen,' Jessie explained. 'She said she'd dye some shoes to match the dress — and she's going to put some of the Cinderella crystals on them too!'

'Oh wow!' I sighed. This was getting better and better!

Being fitted for the dress was just like when I'd seen dancers being fitted for their costumes. Belinda and Jessie used a tape measure to take measurements of me and then scribbled things down on a piece of paper. Then, as I got dressed, Belinda began to trace a pattern of my dress onto paper. She was so quick!

I'd barely put my clothes on when Jessie started to cut out the paper pieces and then she and Belinda sewed them onto some cotton fabric.

'That's not the material I chose though,' I said, disappointed that I wasn't going to get my beautiful floaty dress after all.

'Don't worry,' said Belinda. 'We're going to make a basic dress called a *toile* first. We use that to make sure the size and fitting is absolutely right and then we'll cut another version of the dress out of the real fabric.'

I was mesmerised as I watched Belinda and Jessie use their sewing machines to whiz the seams of the cotton together.

'Come on,' Jessie said. 'School uniform off again – let's see how this fits!'

I jumped up and did as they said. I felt like Cinderella being dressed for the ball as Jessie slipped the cotton dress over my head.

'Do a twirl for us, Tilly!' Jessie asked after she'd pinned the *toile* together at the back.

'It fits perfectly,' I sighed.

I'd just taken off the *toile* when Gerda arrived.

'I've heard all about your dress,' she said. 'What colours have you chosen, Tilly?'

I showed her the fabric and the drawing.

'Fabulous,' said Gerda. 'Here . . .' She took some beautiful satin shoes out of a bag. They were like ballet shoes only they had very tiny heels and a strap across the front.

I tried them on. They were a perfect fit!

'They're beautiful!' I sighed. 'Thank you – thanks, all of you!'

I was so excited about my dress I thought I might burst. I couldn't stop telling Mum and Dad all about it. I even rang Rose as soon as we got home. And, as I twirled around the living room, rehearsing my exam dance, I imagined I was wearing my gorgeous new dress as I moved. And, that night, when I was tucked up in bed with Myrtha, I told her all about it too! But, I wondered, even though Jessie was amazing at sewing things, would it, like my dance, really be ready in time for Saturday . . . ?

Chapter Thirteen

I needn't have worried. The minute I stepped inside the ballet wardrobe the following afternoon, I saw my new dress hanging up. It was nearly finished!

'Gosh!' I gasped, touching the soft fabric with my fingers. It not only looked beautiful, it felt beautiful as well.

'Miaow!' The familiar cry interrupted my thoughts.

'Giselle!' I said, looking around the room. 'Where is she?'

There was a light scratching on the door.

'Oh that's just her way of telling us she would like to be let in!' said Adam, opening the door.

'Miaow!' Giselle announced again before slowly strolling into the room.

'Where have you been?' I asked, scooping her up and giving her a cuddle.

Giselle rubbed her face into my hand and purred contentedly.

'She's probably been down to the scenery department again,' Jessie giggled.

Belinda and Adam laughed.

'Adam found her there yesterday – she was having a snooze inside Cinderella's coach!' said Jessie.

'How did she get there?' I laughed.

'She must have been having a look round and then Harry shut the door without realising she was inside,' Adam said. 'Imagine if she did that on the night of a performance!'

'Wasn't she upset?' I asked.

'She was just curled up asleep,' Jessie said. 'I think she's hungry now. Would you like to give her some food?'

While Giselle was busy eating and Jessie tidied up the worktable, I stood in my dress so Belinda could do the hem.

'Don't you look pretty?' Jessie said. But before I could answer, Mary rushed into the ballet wardrobe.

'Have you heard the news?' she said, anxiously.

'No,' Jessie looked up from her sewing. 'What's happened?'

'Julia's twisted her ankle! She's one of the soloists in *Cinderella*. A fairy. They say she won't be able to dance for at least a week!'

We all gasped. This was terrible news.

'But who's going to take her place?' I asked.

'Mia!' Mary announced. 'She's Julia's understudy. She's going on stage tonight, and there are only two performances until the Gala show!'

Mia had only been a dancer with the Grand Ballet for a short time. Before that she was an Extra, just like me. Mia had taken part in other shows, but always as a member of the *corps de ballet*. She'd never danced a solo before! And now she was going to have to perfect the steps of her dance really quickly. She must feel terrified!

I told Rose what had happened the next day.

'Poor Julia,' I said. 'But isn't it great for

Mia? It's her chance to show everyone just how good she is.'

'I know. I can't believe she's a proper ballerina already! Do you think we'll be like that one day?' Rose wondered.

'Wouldn't it be amazing?' I sighed. *Only ballerinas don't go wrong on stage*, I thought. *Or in their exams.*

'Mia must be really nervous,' said Rose. 'The Gala show's a really important event. It's like us and our ballet exam – only ten times worse!'

'Just thinking about it gives me butterflies,' I agreed.

'We've got our final rehearsal this afternoon!' said Rose.

'Yes,' I said, slipping my arm into hers. 'And this time I've got to get my dance perfect! Just like Mia!'

Chapter Fourteen

Helen collected me and Rose from school and took us straight to Miss Nancy's. We quickly got changed even though there was lots of time before our exam rehearsal began.

At Miss Nancy's, the changing room is actually an area that's sectioned off from the studio with a curtain. On the other side of the curtain, we could hear the pianist playing for the girls who were rehearsing.

'Shall we look through?' Rose suggested.

In some ways, the rehearsal is a bit like doing class. But in it Miss Nancy pretends to be the examiner and talks to us just like they will. And she doesn't give us as many tips as she usually does because she wants us to remember everything for ourselves. Like we have to do in the exam.

Rose pulled back one of the curtains. Just a little bit. She peeped through.

'Move over,' I squeezed in next to Rose and peeped with her.

There were four girls in the studio. All were from our class, and they were good. Unlike me, they didn't seem nervous at all.

We watched them in silence. And then, suddenly, they were doing their *reverence* and their rehearsal was over.

'Come on – it's our turn now!' said Rose.

I followed Rose, along with Sophie and

Chloe, the girls we were doing our exam with, into the studio.

'Ready?' Miss Nancy asked. 'Take your positions at the *barre*, please.'

And then our class began. I concentrated hard and, when we turned round at the *barre* and I caught sight of Rose, I could see she was doing the same.

I did all the things Miss Nancy was always telling us. I had to get everything perfect! I pulled up that imaginary string that came out of the top of my head so I stood really tall! I made sure my shoulders weren't hunched around my ears. I turned out my knees when I was in first position and made sure that they were straight and not leaving space for the sun to shine through. And I pointed my toes so hard they hurt!

'Now, girls, would you do your dance

two at a time, please?' Miss Nancy asked. 'Sophie and Chloe – I'd like you to go first.'

They took their positions. Tinkle, tinkle – the opening chords of the music began. Off they set. They were good! When they'd finished, Rose squeezed my hand and smiled at me. I didn't feel like smiling. I just wanted to run away. But I couldn't. The music had started.

Off we set, skipping and galloping. We mimed listening to the bird that we could hear. We beckoned the bird onto our fingers. But, as the bird flew off, we were meant to dance around using the whole of the studio to catch up with it again. Off we set. Only Rose went one way, and I went the other! Too late! I realised I'd gone in the wrong direction!

What should I do? Should I go back? I didn't know. So I carried on, going the wrong way but doing the correct steps (at least I'd got that bit right for once). It was like Rose and I were doing a circle. We met back in the middle of the room, stepped to the side and pointed our toes in front, the imaginary bird landing on our fingers. And the music stopped.

My face burned red! I'd been a disaster again! Miss Nancy was going to be furious! But she said nothing until Sophie and Chloe came back into the centre and we did our *reverence*. Then she spoke at last.

'Well done, girls,' she said. 'You all did very well.'

'But my dance!' Tears stung my eyes. 'I still haven't got it right!'

'It was only a little bit wobbly,' Miss Nancy said, coming over. 'But the good bit – the excellent bit – was that you carried on! It looked like you were meant to go that way.'

'Really?' I whispered.

'Yes,' Miss Nancy smiled. 'The trick is to look confident and carry on. Just like you did. So well done!'

I smiled a little bit. 'Thank you,' I said.

'And the rest of you were excellent, too,' said Miss Nancy. 'Now, don't worry. It will all be fine tomorrow. Just you wait and see!'

Much later, after Mum had got home, I sat on the sofa and hugged Myrtha. I still felt really stupid about my dance. I understood what Miss Nancy said, but I knew I hadn't been getting better. Perhaps I wasn't ready for the exam . . . I was glad that Mum was there. Because the Gala show was the following night, other dancers were dancing the lead roles in *Cinderella* to give Mum and Dad a small rest.

'Is something wrong?' Mum asked, coming into the room and sitting down next to me.

I shook my head. I was too embarrassed to tell her. I bet she never went wrong with her steps! I snuggled into Myrtha who purred gently.

'Sure?' Mum said, stroking Myrtha as well.

And then it all came out. Everything.

I sniffed and Mum wiped away my tears with her hankie.

'Oh that's happened to me lots of times,' Mum said.

'It has?' I didn't believe her.

'Like Miss Nancy says – keep smiling and look confident. The audience won't know you've made a mistake!' Mum hugged me.

'I bet Mia has learned all her steps,' I said, twiddling Myrtha's tail.

'Well, she's not perfect yet,' Mum said. 'But she's getting there – just like you will.'

'Tomorrow is going to be a scary day for both of us!' I sighed.

'A big day, yes,' said Mum. 'But not scary. You're both going to be brilliant.'

I really hoped she was right!

Chapter Fifteen

Later that night, Dad came and tucked me up in bed. Myrtha was in her usual place curled around my feet.

'Don't you look wonderful on that poster,' he said.

I nodded. I loved my poster.

'Well that's how you're going to be in your exam,' said Dad.

I smiled at him. 'I'll do my best,' I said.

Dad kissed me on the top of my head.

'Of course you will. But now you must

get some sleep so that you feel full of energy in the morning. Night, darling.'

'Night,' I yawned.

After Dad went downstairs, I shut my eyes but I couldn't sleep straightaway. I thought about my exam. And my dance. In my head, I started to hum the music and imagined myself dancing to it. *One, two, three . . . two, two, three . . .* I got to the end without a mistake! If only I could do that tomorrow . . .

Early the next morning, Gran came round to look after me.

'Break a leg!' said Mum and Dad as they left for the theatre to prepare for their own important day. 'You'll be great, Tilly!'

'You too!' I said.

'Now,' asked Gran, shutting the door.

'Is everything ready for your exam? Shall we check?'

Shoes, leotard, tights, hair stuff – everything was in my bag.

'I'll do your hair after you've got dressed,' said Gran. 'That way it will be perfect.'

'Is that what you used to do for Mum?' I asked.

Gran nodded. 'Yes, she used to get herself in a terrible state before exams.'

'Really?' I couldn't imagine Mum, who was just so brilliant at dancing, ever being that nervous.

'Of course,' said Gran. 'I remember one time she just couldn't learn some of her centre work and she was convinced she'd get it wrong in the exam.'

'Did she?' I wondered.

Gran shook her head. 'Not at all,' she said. 'And neither will you!'

On exam days, Miss Nancy always arranged for us to use a different part of the building as a changing room to make things in the studio as quiet as possible. I met Rose there and she was already getting ready. Chloe and Sophie were with her.

'Don't worry,' said Gran. 'You have plenty of time – don't panic!'

'There,' said Helen, when we had finished. 'Don't you both look beautiful?'

It was cold and I hugged my arms around myself as the butterflies began to flutter again. But I couldn't be nervous for long. Seconds later, Miss Nancy appeared in the door.

'Ready, girls?' she smiled. 'Come on – the others have nearly finished. Let's go and listen for the bell!'

The examiner was really friendly and smiled a lot. She made us feel better straightaway. First she checked our names and then she asked us to take our places at the *barre*.

'Now then, girls,' she smiled. 'If you're ready, I'd like to see your *pliés*.'

The exam had begun!

I concentrated hard, listening to the music and interpreting it with my head and arms, just like Miss Nancy always said. As we moved through all our *barre* exercises, I made sure my knees weren't sagging forward and my back was straight. Time flew by and soon we were doing our centre work. I smiled and remembered to look in the right directions when we did our *port de bras*. I jumped as lightly as I could, trying not to sound like an elephant. Then, suddenly, it was time for our dance.

Chloe and Sophie went first, while Rose and I stood as still and as quietly as we could at the side of the studio. Then it was our turn. Rose and I took our places and I took a deep breath.

Please, I thought. *Please let me get it right!*

The music started and we were off. I moved across the studio as lightly as I could. Then, when I got to the bit where I kept going wrong, I followed Rose. And this time it was perfect!

At the end we both stepped to the side and pointed our toes, holding up our hand for our imaginary bird.

'Thank you, girls,' the examiner smiled. 'That was lovely. Now, if you could all gather together, I'd like to see your *reverence* please.'

And that was it. We curtsied, thanked the examiner and the pianist and off we went.

'Phew!' I said to Gran, flopping down on a chair next to her.

'OK?' she asked. The other girls' mums were looking anxious too.

Rose, Chloe, Sophie and I looked at them and grinned.

'Very OK!' we said.

Chapter Sixteen

Rose and I had to hurry to get to our Extras class on time. When we arrived at the Stage Door we quickly waved hello to Bob and sped along the corridor to the changing room.

'Everyone's already gone into the studio!' Rose exclaimed.

'Miss Marion knows we had an exam,' I said, pulling on my ballet shoes. 'She'll understand.'

The music had already begun as we

tiptoed into the studio, slipped into position at the *barre* and started class.

From across the room, Veronica glared at us and raised her snooty nose in the air. That's when I saw Karina. I noticed she'd found herself a place on the *barre* a long way from Veronica. And she didn't glare at me and Rose. No. Karina just smiled and bent into her first *plié*.

I don't know about Rose, but I felt quite tired doing another ballet class after our exam. It felt good though to be able to relax and enjoy dancing without having to worry about remembering the steps.

Afterwards, there was no chance to apologise to Miss Marion because she was busy talking to the pianist.

'Don't worry,' I said to Rose as we

headed back to the changing room. 'I'm sure she will have remembered that we were going to be late.'

As soon as we'd got through the door, Veronica leapt on us.

'Fancy turning up so late for class!' she snapped.

'But –' Rose tried to explain.

Veronica didn't let her finish. 'Real dancers would *never* do that!' she ranted. 'It's so unprofessional!'

Karina, who was sitting on the bench changing out of her shoes, gasped. She opened her mouth, about to speak, but Veronica kept going on about how dancers had to be committed to dance and that nothing should ever make them late for class.

I was about to tell Rose to ignore her when Miss Marion swept into the changing room. Veronica immediately put on a sickly sweet smile. Honestly – that girl is unbelievable!

But Miss Marion didn't seem to see her. Instead, she came straight over to us.

'How did your exam go?' she asked, anxiously.

'We did all our exercises right,' said Rose.

'And we didn't make any mistakes in our dance,' I confirmed.

'Excellent,' Miss Marion smiled. 'Don't forget to let me know as soon as you hear your results. Now, did someone say you'll be at the Gala show this evening?'

We nodded, excitedly.

'Well, have a wonderful time,' Miss Marion said. 'Maybe I'll see you there! Bye, everyone!'

'Goodbye, Miss Marion,' Veronica replied the loudest. 'And thank you!'

Miss Marion swished out of the room. But she'd hardly left when Veronica turned on us again.

'You're going to the Gala show?' she hissed.

We nodded.

'Well you'd better behave properly at that!' she huffed, turning her back on us.

I rolled my eyes at Rose and we giggled.

'Miaowww!'

Giselle! She was sitting on top of my ballet bag.

'She must have been waiting for you,' said Rose. 'How did she know you were here?'

I shrugged. After nuzzling Rose as she finished getting dressed, Giselle moved off to inspect the rest of the changing room. She headed straight for Veronica.

'Get away! Get off, you disgusting thing!' she yelped, pushing her roughly away.

I raced over to pick up Giselle.

'Don't be so mean!' Karina said to Veronica.

Veronica looked at her, clearly shocked.

'I . . . I . . . I thought it was a mouse or something,' she spluttered.

'Well it's a dear little cat,' Karina said. 'She won't do you any harm.'

Karina came over and stroked Giselle.

'Isn't she beautiful,' she said. 'Does she live here?'

Then Rose and I told Karina the whole story. How Giselle had been found hiding in the theatre and how she'd been named after the ballet that was being performed at the time.

'That's so sweet,' Karina said.

Veronica just glared at us. Like her eyes would pop out!

'Come on,' Rose said. 'We'd better hurry or my mum and your gran will be wondering where we are!'

'Yes,' said Karina. 'I've got to rush too. But I heard you say you were going to the Gala show this evening.'

'That's right,' we said.

'So am I,' Karina said. 'Maybe I'll see you there!'

Chapter Seventeen

Much later that afternoon, Gran and I set off for the Grand Theatre, ready for the Gala show. Still dressed in my jeans, I felt a bit out of place next to Gran who was looking super smart in a beautiful dress. Still – soon I was going to be wearing my very own special dress, wasn't I?

The theatre was already buzzing with excitement and activity. We were going to meet Helen and Rose inside after I'd handed over the bouquet to Madame

Satina. But Gran and I went round to the Stage Door.

'Hi, Bob!' I said as we went to find Jessie.

'Good luck with your bouquet thing!' Bob grinned as he let us through.

In the ballet wardrobe, Gran made a huge fuss of Giselle as Jessie helped me change. While she did, I told her all about my exam.

'I said it would be OK!' Jessie smiled, putting the dress over my head.

It felt swishy and special and shimmered in the light.

'I found these tights for you,' said Belinda, handing me a pair that were exactly the right colour for the dress.

'Thanks!' I said, pulling them on.

'And here are your shoes,' said Adam, taking them out of the box for me. 'Let's see what you look like!'

I slipped them on and did them up. I couldn't resist doing a twirl.

'Now what's happening about your hair?' asked Jessie.

'Tilly's mum thought it should hang loose and be held back with this headband,' said Gran. 'She found it specially.'

I peeked in the mirror. The headband was a lovely surprise and it was really pretty. I glanced up and down at my reflection. I'd never seen myself in such a fancy outfit before.

'Miaoww!' purred Giselle.

'Perfect,' said Jessie.

And everyone else agreed.

Just then, there was an announcement from the stage manager over the loud speaker, telling people how long there was before the performance started.

'We'd better go,' said Gran.

She took my hand and led me along the corridor. Turning a corner, we nearly bumped into someone. It was a fairy in a tutu that looked like it had been sprinkled in glitter.

'Mia!' I said. 'You look amazing!' Even her pointe shoes were silver!

Dressed in her costume, Mia looked really nervous. And for the second time that day, I too had butterflies in my tummy. Though I don't know why. Giving a bunch of flowers to someone isn't nearly as terrifying as doing a solo on a stage in front of hundreds of people.

'Hi, Tilly,' Mia said. 'And I love *your* dress! Are you off to meet Madame Satina?'

I nodded. 'Good luck for tonight!' I said quietly.

Mia smiled. 'Thanks – good luck to you too! Now, I've got to rush. I need to warm up at the *barre*.'

Gran and I made our way to the foyer. It was jam packed with people. Including some with cameras! More people and photographers were outside on the steps.

'I hadn't realised Madame Satina would be so popular,' I said to Gran.

'She's a very important lady in the world of ballet,' Gran explained.

'Hello,' said Antonia, rushing up as soon as she saw us. 'Tilly, don't you look gorgeous! Now . . .' She was talking so fast I didn't get the chance to reply. 'Here . . .' Antonia thrust a beautiful bouquet at me. 'These are for Madame Satina. She'll be arriving in a few minutes and I'll be there to meet her. Then, after I've walked with her up the steps, perhaps you could step forward and present the bouquet?'

I nodded.

'Excellent,' said Antonia. 'Good luck!'

Holding tight to Gran's hand, I glanced around. The theatre foyer was looking even more amazing than usual. It had been decorated for Christmas with an enormous Christmas tree laden with sparkling lights and decorations. Suddenly, a great cheer came up from the crowd. There were flashes of light from the cameras.

'It's Madame Satina's car!' announced Antonia. 'Ready, Tilly?'

'Yes,' I grinned, clutching the flowers, though the butterflies in my tummy were going crazy.

'I'll just wait over there with Jessie,' said Gran, leaving me at the top of the steps.

I glanced over to Gran, who was now standing back by the theatre doors. Jessie gave me the thumbs up. I hadn't realised that she'd be here too!

The crowd were clapping now. I turned and saw Madame Satina getting out of the car. She was wearing a long blue dress. She looked beautiful – so graceful and elegant as she chatted to Antonia. Flash, flash went the cameras. I watched as Madame Satina came up the steps and started to talk to all the people who were waiting to see her. And that's when I saw Giselle!

Chapter Eighteen

Honestly! It was Giselle! And she was calmly walking towards me!

She didn't seem to be at all worried about the crowd. Or the lights from the cameras, which were flashing away.

'Miaowwww!' Giselle announced as she stopped in front of me.

'Come on, Giselle,' I whispered. 'Come here.'

I was trying to make her move out of the way. But the photographers had caught sight of Giselle and started to take her photograph! Giselle seemed to love being in the limelight and started to do one of her tiptoe dances for them.

But then, all at once, Antonia was walking towards me with Madame Satina. Giselle took one look at them and began to miaow louder than ever, as if she was speaking to them.

'Oh,' said Antonia and then she smiled. 'Madame, this is our theatre cat, Giselle. And this is Chantilly Tippington.'

I bobbed my best curtsey ever, smiled and offered the bouquet to Madame Satina.

'Hello, Chantilly,' said Madame. 'And Giselle. I've heard lots about both of you.' *She had? Madame Satina knew who I was?* She took a sniff of her flowers. 'These are gorgeous – thank you, Tilly. And what a beautiful dress you're wearing – it reminds me of a costume I once wore. How lovely!'

Wow, I thought. *Perhaps she was the dancer in the dress I saw at the museum!*

Madame Satina smiled at me and then said, 'Are you here to see your parents this evening, Chantilly?'

'Yes,' I nodded. 'And my friend Mia is one of the fairies – it's her first dance as a soloist!'

'Well I shall look out for her then!' said Madame. 'Thank you – and enjoy the show. I've very much enjoyed meeting you. And Giselle too!'

And just as quickly as she'd arrived, Madame Satina was gone.

'Well done, Tilly!' said Jessie, rushing over to me with Gran.

'Yes,' said Gran. 'I loved your curtsey. Now, we'd better take our seats – it's nearly time for curtain up!'

'And I think I'd better get Giselle backstage again!' giggled Jessie, scooping her up.

Rose and Helen waved excitedly as we appeared in the stalls.

'How did it go?' Rose asked.

'It was amazing,' I said. 'Madame is so

friendly. And Giselle came to meet her too!'

'No way!' Rose giggled.

'Yes,' I laughed. 'Madame stroked Giselle and everything. She even knew all about her!'

'Look!' said Rose. 'Karina's over there! She's waving!'

We looked up to the balcony seats and waved back, smiling.

'And isn't that Veronica over there too?' whispered Rose as the lights dimmed.

Veronica was gawping at us through the increasing gloom. I waved at her. But she didn't wave back. And then the audience hushed as the conductor entered the orchestra pit and the music began. *Cinderella*'s gala performance was about to start.

From the opening scenes with Cinderella (my mum!), lonely in the kitchen being bossed about by her horrible sisters, right through to the moment when those same sisters were getting ready to go to the ball, I was enchanted.

'For one awful moment I thought they were going to change the story and Cinderella was *not* going to go to the ball!' said Rose, when the lights went up for the interval.

'I was so relieved when I saw the Fairy Godmother come on stage!' I agreed.

'Sorry to interrupt,' said Gran, 'but does anyone fancy an ice cream?'

'Yes, please!' Rose and I said together.

Gran gave us some money and we went off to find one. Unfortunately, we also found Veronica. There she was at the front of the line.

'Hello, Veronica,' I said. 'Are you enjoying the ballet?'

Veronica turned round and gave us one of her usual glares.

'Oh no, not you two dweebs,' she sighed. 'And what *are* you wearing?'

'The cheek . . .' I began.

But Veronica turned round, paid for her ice cream and then shoved us out of her way. 'Move!' she snapped.

'Why does she always have to be like this?' Rose wondered.

'Beats me,' I giggled. 'But I do know that I'd like a chocolate ice cream!'

Chapter Nineteen

In the next act, Snowdrop, the pony I'd been told about, came on! She trotted across the stage, taking Cinderella to the ball. Everyone clapped. My mum looked gorgeous in her costume. And the ball scene was just wonderful with all the sparkly costumes and the fabulous ballroom that they had made out of painted panels.

As Cinderella danced in her crystal slippers with my handsome Dad, I looked down at my own crystal-encrusted shoes that were twinkling under the theatre lights.

As the music swept the dancers away, I tapped my fingers to the beat. I must have read the story of Cinderella a hundred times but I still couldn't help wanting to shout out when the clock struck midnight.

Rose and I held each other's hands as Cinderella panicked and left the ball! The act ended with Cinderella fleeing in the coach, which disappeared in a puff of smoke. It was magical – just like my mum and dad's dancing. I was so proud of them!

The final act of *Cinderella* was even better than the rest. Mia had a big dance that she had to do with the other fairies, as well as her own solo part. And she really was like a fairy – flittering around on her toes, light as a feather. I hoped that she'd remember her steps and I crossed my fingers for her as she pirouetted around the stage. I needn't have been nervous though! Mia's footwork was perfect. And her eyes sparkled as she danced, spreading the magic through her steps and along her fairy wand. The audience burst into applause when she'd finished! I wanted to be a ballerina like

Mia! I wanted to dance with her now! But then, having spun their magic, the fairies flew off the stage. And before we knew it, Cinderella and Prince Charming were getting married. The ballet was over and the curtain fell.

The whole theatre erupted with applause.

'That was amazing,' Rose and I agreed.

As the dancers took their *reverence*, we clapped so hard that our hands hurt.

'Look!' said Rose, pointing up towards the balcony.

Madame Satina was smiling and clapping. She even stood up from her seat.

'She obviously enjoyed it as much as we did!' I grinned.

We started to make our way out of the stalls, on our way to see Mum and Dad, when Rose and I felt taps on our shoulders. It was Karina!

'Hello, you two,' she smiled. 'I loved the ballet, didn't you?'

'Oh yes. It was amazing,' Rose said.

'And is it true that your mum and dad were dancing the lead roles, Tilly?' Karina asked.

'Yes,' I said, proudly.

'And our friend Mia was one of the fairies,' Rose pointed out. 'She used to be in Extras with us! And now she's already had a solo part!'

'I hope I'm good enough to dance on stage one day,' Karina sighed.

'I'm sure you will.' I said. 'You're the best dancer in the class,'

'Definitely,' Rose nodded.

'Thanks,' Karina said modestly. 'But I've still got lots to learn. Er, listen . . . this is a bit embarrassing. And probably none of my business. But I saw you at the interval.

I heard what Veronica said. About how you looked and stuff.'

'Oh yeah,' I said. 'That's typical. She's always saying things like that.'

'Well it was horrible,' said Karina. 'She shouldn't speak to you like that. And I'm going to tell her so when I see her at Extras.'

'Oh,' said Rose. Neither of us could imagine what Veronica would make of someone telling her off. Especially Karina.

'Anyway,' Karina said. 'I'd better get back to my parents. See you both next week.'

'Yes,' we nodded. 'Bye!'

'Wow,' I said, turning to Rose. 'Fancy that. We'd better make sure we get to Extras early next week. We don't want to miss Veronica getting put in her place!'

Chapter Twenty

I couldn't stop thinking about *Cinderella*.
I could hear the music in my head as I
whirled and pirouetted around the house
all day on Sunday. And when Gran
suggested we made some Christmas cards,
I used Cinderella's story as my inspiration!

After school the next day, Dad took
me straight to the theatre and dropped
me off at the ballet wardrobe. There was
no performance that night, and I was
glad we'd be able to spend the evening
together.

'Mum and I will be finished in a tick,' he explained. 'See you soon!'

I pushed open the big red doors. Jessie, Belinda, and Adam were inside, drinking tea and reading the newspaper.

'Hello!' I called.

'Tilly!' Jessie said. 'That's good timing. Come and see this!'

She pointed to the front page of the newspaper. I sat on a stool next to her and looked. It was me! And Giselle! A photo of me and Giselle speaking to Madame Satina!

'Oh wow!' I said. 'I don't believe it!'

Just then, Giselle jumped up onto the worktable, walked straight over to the newspaper, which was spread out on the top, and curled up on it, purring.

We all laughed.

'Isn't this brilliant?' Jessie said, after

she'd read it out, around Giselle's fur. As well as being about Madame Satina, it also said how Giselle had come to live in the theatre. And there was even something about Mum, Dad and me. 'You'll have to keep it as a souvenir.'

I grinned. Nothing like this had happened to me before.

'I'm going to put it in my special tin!' I said.

My special tin had been given to me by Jessie. It had a picture of a ballerina on the front and I kept special ballet memories in it. Like sequins from some costumes, and programmes from performances I'd seen.

'That's the perfect place to keep it,' Jessie said. 'And when Giselle wakes up, you can show it to your mum and dad. But right now, I've got something for us to do together. Look!'

Jessie took a basket from the cupboard and brought it to the worktable.

'There!' She took out two cat collars.

'What are we going to do with those?' I asked.

'I thought we could decorate them!' Jessie grinned. She showed me a bag of crystals, just like the ones on my special Gala shoes. And like the ones on Cinderella's costumes.

'Cool!' I said. 'One for Giselle and one for Myrtha!'

'Exactly,' Jessie agreed.

As Adam and Belinda started work again, Jessie and I got creative too. It was really good fun choosing colours and deciding on which patterns to put the crystals in. And Jessie had a special glue pen that made them stick. Giselle purred and kept looking at what we were doing.

'There!' Jessie said, looking at our

finished collars. 'We'll need to leave them to dry and then our furry friends can wear them.'

Everyone was admiring the collars when Mum and Dad burst into the room.

'Tilly!' said Dad 'We've got some great news!'

'Have you seen the paper?' I asked.

'No,' said Mum. 'What does it say?'

So Jessie and I showed Mum and Dad the article in the newspaper.

'Isn't that terrific!' said Dad.

'Amazing,' agreed Mum. 'But that's not what we were going to tell you!'

'No,' said Dad. 'It's about your exam!'

'I've just had a phone call from Miss Nancy,' explained Mum. 'She's received the results from the examiner.'

'Already?' I whispered.

I'd only taken my exam a couple of

days before. I hadn't realised I would get
the result so quickly. I felt those butterflies
in my tummy again. Had I passed? I felt a
bit sick.

'Don't look so worried!' Mum hugged
me. 'It's OK.'

'OK?' said Dad. 'It's more than OK!
Tilly – you got Honours! You *and* Rose!
You *both* got Honours!'

And he scooped me up in his arms and twirled me around.

Honours! Me *and* Rose! We'd both got top marks!

'How fantastic is that?' said Jessie, giving me another hug.

'Miaow!' said Giselle, joining in the excitement.

Later that night, tucked up in bed with Myrtha. I looked up at the poster on my wall. Not for the first time, I imagined that it really was me in the tutu, twirling around the stage. Me, a real ballerina. I desperately hoped it would happen. And, now that I'd got Honours in my exam, I wondered if it might . . .

Look out for more adventures starring
Tilly Tiptoes and all her friends
at the Grand Ballet

Tilly Tiptoes
and the
Grand Surprise

The dancers of the Grand Ballet are
practising for the opening night of *Giselle*.
But objects are going missing from the
theatre, from bits of costume to leotards
and legwarmers. Is there a naughty fairy
up to no good, or maybe even a ghost?
Tilly tries to find out . . .

Tilly Tiptoes
takes a
Curtain Call

Tilly and Rose have the chance in a
lifetime. They are auditioning for a ballet
that will be shown at the Grand Theatre!
But Tilly has been given thirteen as her
audition number and now everything
keeps going wrong. Can she stop the
jinx to get her first lucky break?